The Poets and the Assassin

By Reza Jalali

D1714951

Refuge is an original work of art by Niyaz Azadikhah and is used here with her permission.

All poems in this book are translated by the Author.

Contents

Also by Reza Jalali

Moon Watchers: Shirin's Ramadan Miracle

Homesick Mosque and Other Stories

For Jaleh, Setareh, and women in Iran.

Introduction

Memories. The kind that stays with you for life and capture all your senses: the stories, sighs, laughter, tears, dancing, cooking, the aroma of spices, singing, and whispers. These are the memories I still recall of the women—relations or strangers—who helped me see the world through their eyes, as I grew up in a dusty border town in the Kurdish region of Iran. They are sad, happy and magical memories: my eldest sister, Baji, horseback riding when in her teens in the 1940's, riding from one village to another, in Iranian Kurdistan. I picture her flying through the landscape like a furious female warrior from the 10th century Persian epic, *Shah-nameh*, The Book of Kings. I watched our widowed neighbor, Mim-Ezat, raising three children on wages she earned washing people's clothes, after her husband, a smuggler, was shot dead by the Iranian border police, the *gendarmes*. The women around me inspired, mesmerized, and frightened me. Some had magic: I watched babies born at home—our town had no hospital but a clinic—and how women had the gift to both create life and bring a child into this world. They had power: the old healers, whose touch mended broken bones, and hearts, whose words saved marriages and sharp tongues made the town's men behave. When younger, and still tolerated as part of the tribe of the women, I watched them wait for the men to leave the house, to start dancing, raising their arms toward the sky and moving their hips seductively, to the music from the radio. On family outings in the summertime, we picnicked on a family-owned fruit orchard that bordered a river with cool, emerald-green water. The younger kids stood guard to keep away the unwanted gazes, as the women, taking advantage of the men's customary afternoon naps, went in for a dip in the river, shaded and hidden by the palms and mulberry trees, in their underwear.

I heard whispers: young leftist and nationalist Kurdish women, *peshmerga* fighters, taking arms and dying in the mountains of Kurdistan. I wept hearing sentimental poetry praising them that was written by the old Kurdish poets. I felt sad and confused when my pretty sister was coerced to marry her first cousin, since my sweet but traditional mother insisted, in keeping with the land's culture, on having one of her daughters marry her nephew. Some protested on my sister's behalf: my physicist brother, Ahmad, pleaded with our mother. For years to follow, the same sister stayed in the abusive marriage for the sake of her kids, and the family's honor.

I heard sighs: my mother spoke with longing of distant lands, and cities that shined at nights with lights, which she might never get to see but her sons would visit; I saw my own sisters working hard as teachers and waiting for a 'good' man to marry, in order to find happiness. It was fun to be a boy; it was easy to come and go and do the things the girls could not do. When I was ten or eleven, my parents bought me a Swiss-made wristwatch. I knew my sister, older than me by few years, had asked for one for a long time. I felt embarrassed whenever I saw her looks of longing at my shiny watch. In a month or two, my watch was stolen at school. Did I misplace it subconsciously to correct the injustice? I still wonder.

Looking back, I realize, with yearning, that I was raised and surrounded by the fearless *shir-zan*, lion-hearted, women of Kurdistan and Iran. You could say my education started early and well.

****

The story of Iranian women, including their century-old battle for rights, remains with the few exceptions, untold. Though they have been in the forefront of the national struggle for independence, liberty and democracy in Iran, and have been among the most educated and most independent women in the Middle East—they entered universities in 1935 and gained the right to vote in 1963—to those in the West, their lives stay, for most part, in purdah, hidden and veiled in mystery. Ironically, their tale is one of courage, resistance, sacrifice, and survival in an intensely traditional and patriarchal society, for unlike some of their sisters, in countries near and far, they have actively participated in the public sphere to protest, ask for rights, and demand equality. For example, during the turbulent 1906 Constitution Revolution, a group of veiled women, fed up with the monarch's efforts to undermine the national movement to bring democracy to Iran, marched to the *majlis,* the Iranian parliament. Once there, with pistols hidden under their *chador*, the one-piece cloth covering the body but leaving the face exposed that traditional Iranian women wear when in public, they threatened to kill their husbands, sons, and themselves, if the parliament were to side with the corrupt king and abandon on its constitutional duties.

Iranian women live complex and complicated lives. Facing the tyranny of outdated traditional practices, religious extremism and a male-dominated political system, they are forced to live multiple identities and lives: one in public and another in private, as they struggle with tension among tradition and modernity and orthodox, and, since the 1979 Islamic Revolution, conservative Shia Islam and secularism.

Why this play? I penned *The Poets and the Assassin* to put a human face on Iranian women, made invisible by those in power and ignored by the indifferent and biased media, and to highlight their historical struggle for rights and human dignity, by telling their story. Most in the West react to women's issues in Iran, or for that matter in Muslim societies, by blaming Islam and suggesting a one-size-fits-all remedy, not realizing that Islam is not the problem, not realizing that feminism can take many forms. The black and white, here-or-there explanation is a false one. The story of Iranian women, similar to the elaborate and intricate designs of the world-famous Persian carpets, is colorful, puzzling, and filled with mystery. Shia Islam might have a part in the chaotic puzzle of the treatment of Iranian women, but additionally there are the cultural, traditional, tribal, and political factors that are as responsible. For instance, when it comes to *hejab*, the veil, it is, contrary to the popular belief, shared even by some Iranians, a pre-Islamic practice. Persian kings and members of the royal family and the society's aristocrats were known to cover their faces when in public, perhaps to block the evil eye. My hope: the play might help to create an accurate picture of Iranian women by challenging our assumptions about them. A myth-buster, it makes us see them for who they are: fearless *shir-zan*, fighting oppression and tyranny—a battle that can be ours, as well.

Borrowing the Iranian women's famed and loved progenitor, Scheherazade's opening words that saved her life and that of her sisters to come: "let me tell you their story…"

Reza Jalali, 2015

Cast of Characters

DAUGHTER OF IRAN: A woman of any age

SHAHEREZADE, THE STORY TELLER: A young woman

THE MERMAIDS AND… : A woman of any age

THE VEIL THINGY: A woman of any age

THE ASSASSIN: A young woman

Act I
The Daughter of Iran

The DAUGHTER OF IRAN walks to the center of the stage, smiles and addresses the audience.

WOMAN: WOMAN: My name is Iran-dokht, the daughter of Iran. My story would be different if I were born a boy child and were the son-of-Iran. My gender is my curse. It defines me and limits what I can do and cannot do, what I can say or cannot say. My womanhood makes me invisible, mysterious, while a soft target for the many intolerant men in my culture and religion. I am a woman born in Iran. I've survived upheavals, invasions, occupations, and revolutions. I'm at once a Persian Zoroastrian, following this ancient religion that requires good thoughts, good words, and good deeds from its followers, or an Iranian Muslim, a Shia, who is inspired by Fatima, the Prophet Mohammed's daughter, and taught to suffer and struggle in life, as she did. I can be traditional, modern, religious, or secular. I'm known for my beauty, a curse more than a tribute, in my case, for it has caused my being bought and sold, married off as a child-bride, kidnapped and sent to lands as far away as China, where I was a dance girl, a concubine, during the Tang dynasty. Much has been said about my beauty; the renowned poets of Persia have compared my round face to the moon; my eyes to that of a gazelle; my lips to a ripe pomegranate cut in half; my long black hair to the extended moonless nights of winter; and my slender neck to that of a swan. Many Iranians agree with a

1

popular author who wrote of Iranian women as "life's salt," meaning life without us could be bland and lacking any flavor. Men warn of the sorrow and heartbreak I cause them as I reject their unsolicited love. I live in men's unfulfilled dreams. I torment them with my indifference to their longing. If you ask me... *(She lowers her voice.)* I am a woman, good looks or not, capable of loving and being loved. I need no male guardian. Leave me alone and I'll be fine!

You ask me how old I am? I was born a few thousand years ago, in ancient Persia, when it was a vast empire—a superpower of its era, the same country that changed its name to Iran in the early twentieth century. I might even be one of Cyrus the Great's daughters, a just king who brought freedom to the captive Jews of Babylon, and helped them to rebuild their destroyed temple. Or, a beautiful queen by the name of Esther. I was married to King Xerxes in ancient Persia whose evil prime minister convinced him to kill the land's Jewish population. I saved them all by sharing my secret with my husband that I, too, was a Jew. To this day, Jews everywhere recall my intervention by celebrating the Jewish spring holiday of Purim. I am the Sassanid princess Puran-dokht, who ruled for two years over the Persian Empire. I could be a few hundred years old, born in the majestic city of Isfahan, once Iran's capital city—famous for its stunning mosques, wide boulevards, and its architectural wonders—to a family of Islamic scholars who had me home-schooled so that I could read and write in Farsi and Arabic, recite poetry, and read the

Qur'an, Islam's holy book. You ask me how old I am. I am old enough to remember hearing of Sadigeh Dawlatabadi, representing Iran in the 1926 International Women's Conference in Paris. Men were irate when she came back, unveiled and wearing European outfits! Speaking of unhappy men, I am the singer, the first woman to be on the Iranian National Radio, singing love songs; my voice, carried by the magic of unseen signals to the public teashops and bathhouses, bazaars, and homes, competing for attention with the call to prayer, chanted by old men from the neighborhood mosques. *(The sound of Azan, the Islamic call to pray, mixing with an old-sounding Iranian melody accompanied by a woman vocalist, comes from behind the stage.)* There were death threats sent to the radio station! But I continued to perform for years to come, knowing women in carpet workshops, the homemakers, the young, soon-to-be-brides, would pause and smile once they heard me sing of my sorrow and longing. Other women followed, most using a pseudonym.

I have had my share of misfortune and happiness for being a woman born in a traditional society that is fickle about the role of women. No regrets! I am old and young, a newborn and dying of old age. Still, I could be the daughter of a poor washerwoman, living in the slums of south of Tehran just as the Islamic Revolution of 1997 was unfolding. Indeed, that would make me the daughter of the Islamic Revolution. Possibly my mother was still pregnant with me when she, along with the women of her generation, took to the streets to

3

protest and demand an end to monarchy. *(Her voice becomes excited.)* I still hear their slogans, asking for liberty and bread, dignity and better wages. Risking their lives, marriages, and family relationships, they defeated the Shah's powerful army, sending the king, a dictator, whom the Western governments had long supported, into exile. *(She sighs.)* Maybe I am the daughter of every revolution, every one of which has failed to bring bread and freedom to its mothers, daughters, and sons.

But who cares how old I am? In the West you can be obsessed with age! In the East, where I come from, getting old is seen as a privilege. When we were children, our elders hoped for us to grow to become an adult, to get old, since many never made it past childhood. Age is just a number. Many of my poorer sisters living in countries near and far have no birth certificates; no record of their births were ever kept. Their coming to this world, just as their leaving it, is hardly acknowledged by others. They might be desired when young, to rape, to marry, to mother healthy children, to be recruited for human trafficking, but at times despised and abandoned when old. Age, for most women in my country, is something complex: confusing as one goes from being a child to a woman, worrisome as men start to look at you strangely, shameful, and scary as you age and become an adult. Where was I?

I am ancient, old, young, an infant, and yet to be born. I travelled to the International Space Station, as the first Iranian woman to do so back in 2006. I am Shirin Ebadi, the first

Iranian to receive the Nobel Peace prize! I am related to Maryam Mirzakhani, who became the first woman in the U.S. to be honored with the Fields Medal for mathematics. I'm the daughter of Farrokhroo Parsa, executed by firing squad in 1980 for being a minister in the Shah's government. I am a daughter of Iran, as my name, Iran-dokt, Iran's daughter, suggests. I am a female offspring of the land of the lion and sun, of lovers and roses, of poetry and mysticism, of merciless kings and silenced queens, of misguided bearded men and veiled women, of imprisoned poets and greedy merchants. For some, I am a ghost. For others, I perfume the world with my presence. I exist in every poet's wild imagination while tormenting every religious man's heart, blackened by the fear of God's wrath.

I am the young woman who has been thrown into the beds of old men, fed poison by the jealous first wives, beaten up by mad brothers, accused of adultery and stoned to death, and set on fire, by bearded tyrants. I've been silenced, erased from memories, pushed out of the history books, and denied public space. My image has been removed from painted murals. At times, my children have been told lies that I had died giving birth to them, when in truth had "gone missing" and grown old in mental hospitals. Lately, *(She lowers her voice.)* once again, on orders given by the religious men, who claim to speak for my God, I have been forced to cover myself in black chadors, made to resemble a potato bag... *(Escalating emotionally.)* Now get this! So the men, unrelated to me, would not get

5

excited seeing my hair and body and risk sinning and straying from God's Straight Path. Lately, men whose hearts are untouched with love throw acid on the faces of young women. The nightmare of being a woman being in public continues. *(She pauses. Silence follows. Slowly, with her head down, she unwraps a folded black* chador *and covers herself from head to toe, the way Iranian women wear their chador.)* Since 1997, when bearded men, calling themselves the Soldiers of God, came to power, I have been called the daughter of Islam, Fatima herself, or, a daughter of Imam Ali, the Shia saint and told my bare skin or the loose strands of my hair would make faithful men go mad, forcing them to sin. *(She lowers her voice further to a whisper.)* Between you and me... *(She looks over her shoulder to her right and left and walks closer to the edge.)* One has to be careful these days, for there are government informers everywhere, listening to what is being said and not said. Who wants to be lashed publicly for saying something judged as anti-government? Let me be honest and risk it all, lashes or not: why should I be held liable for men's perceived inability to control their lust? I hate being their sexual gatekeeper! Do I walk around eyeing every man I fancy, picturing them naked and engaged in sex with me? Do I? Hey, it is healthy to control one's impulses! I resist mine, as natural as they are, and men could do the same. Can't they?

These days I am told by the Iranian state-run media that as a Muslim woman, I am the guardian of the dignity of all women; that the covering of my hair and my body would be a thorn in the eye of the enemies of the Iranian government. No pressure! Of course, I could disagree, but nobody cares to listen. *(She sighs.)* The powerful men, who control my society and try to control my mind and body, have the guns and the keys to the prisons. So, I do in public what I am told and do in private what I please.

Where were we? *(She appears thoughtful. Silence. Next she lowers her head, bringing a hand to her face as if wiping a tear.)*

I was telling you who I was and where I came from: I die every time a man hits a woman. Every dawn, I am born once again just as God's gentle fingers place a drop of water, a *shabnam*, night dew, on a rose in the garden. I die every time a young girl's dream is shattered. I come back to life with the sound of flutes played by the lost shepherd and the young girls and boys in the majestic mountains of Kurdistan. I am reborn for the sake of my grandmother, my mother, sisters, and wives of my brothers. I have stories to tell, tears to wipe and collect as keepsakes, sighs to tally, lashes to count, love to give and receive, kisses to plant, and births to give, for I am a woman, maybe a few millennium old, maybe centuries old, born and died in 1979, in a revolution that turned its back on the women who gave it its birth. *(She speaks with confidence.)*

I am a woman who is a pagan, a Zoroastrian, a Jew, an Armenian, an Assyrian Christian, a Muslim, a Baha'i, a nationalist, a leftist, a communist, a secular, a conservative, an atheist, a homemaker, a teacher, a nurse, an engineer, a painter, a poet, an attorney, a political activist, or none of these.

My name is Iran-dokht. Let me tell you my story. *(The lights fade and the stage goes dark. The DAUGHTER OF IRAN leaves the stage.)*

Blackout

End of Act

Act II
Sheherazade, the Storyteller

The stage lights come on. The sound of soft Middle Eastern music can be heard. The character, a young woman, dressed in old Persian-style clothes walks to the center of the stage to address the audience.

SCHEHERAZADE: My name is Scheherazade, and I live in the heart of storytellers everywhere. I am the central character of the fabled One Thousand and One Night stories. In the west, you know me as Scheherazade of the Arabian Nights, and, mistakenly, associate me with belly dancers, snake charmers, and morally-loose black-eyed beauties. A minor case of Orientalism, if you ask me! In my life, I have seduced only one man, a king, by telling him stories: many, many stories, in order to postpone my own death, to survive. Interestingly, once I'm done with telling stories, the guy falls in love with me and we become a husband and wife. Let me tell you Scheherazade's, or, my story from the start: there's this guy, a merciless king, by the name of Shahryar. He has a wife, who betrays him by falling for another man. Now don't ask me how his wife met her lover and dated him, for this thing happened some five or six hundred years ago, before Facebook, twitter, and online matching came to exist! The king is incensed, and vows never to trust a woman again. He comes up with a plan, a deadly one, by which he'd marry a different virgin each night, a beauty whose naked body has not been seen even by sun or moon, never mind touched by a man, every night a new woman to do his business with and have her

9

murdered the very next day. Can you imagine this? *(She giggles.)* This gives the one-night stand a whole different meaning, does it not? The rapist/murderer king goes around marrying one thousand beauties recruited from the land he rules over. Then it is my turn to become his one-night bride. I'd have been the one thousand and first victim. Talk about rotten luck! On the fateful night, I am taken to the royal chamber: bathed, legs shaven, perfumed, made-up and dressed in the finest silk. I sit there wishing I had been born ugly, or, born a few centuries later when I could have used my good looks to land myself a job selling cosmetics at Macy's, or, find a rich dentist to marry me. The handsome king enters the room, looking smug. He looks at me, and I tremble with fear. He sits to eat and asks me to join him. There's a feast: every kinds of choice meat: rare birds, lamb that had been fed the freshest grass of the Zagros mountains; fish from the Caspian Sea, a lake in northern Iran so large it is called a sea; a whole baby lamb stuffed with dried fruit and nuts decorated with stuffed eggplants and green peppers; kebabs of every type, and the Jeweled Rice, named so for the different berries, nuts, and saffron that made it colorful. All of it has been prepared in the royal kitchen and tested for poison by royal food tasters. Silver cups of red wine made from the finest grapes grown in city of Shiraz, and pomegranates, dates, and apricots gathered for the king's wedding night. I have my eyes on the rich *Fesen-jaan*, Food of Life, a stew made with pomegranates and crushed walnut, my favorite. I have fasted all day and am starving. As I help myself to large portions of the Food of Life, with no shame, for the royal etiquette and calories had to wait since I was to die next morning, I cannot help but remember the popular poem that I know by heart:

To Fast and have a frugal life
Was all that I had wished.
But the temptation of the Food Life
Is too much to bear—do not judge me!

The court musicians, all women, for no man would be allowed inside the king's wedding chamber, are busy playing. They might as well be playing my funeral music, I think! I steal a glance at the king and realize we could have made a handsome couple. Chewing on the yummy kebabs, I picture us living in the suburb, having two children, and driving a minivan if only he were not a dangerous serial murderer, pretending to be a bride-groom. This realization makes me lose my appetite. I ask for permission to have a cup of wine. I might as well turn it into a party! The king's eyes shine; he seems surprised. He nods and I gulp down the sweet red wine. By the second cup, I'm not feeling fearful! I recite a poem by the ancient Persian scholar and poet Omar Khayyam, louder than I had intended. I blush and lower my head. The King waves his hand and the room goes silent. "Recite again!" The wine has gone to my pretty head and I try hard to say the words correctly:

Unless we clap hands together in unison,
And dance with joy, we could not end the sorrow
Let us drink from a cup before the dawn
For the morning comes whether we breathe or not!

11

The King seems thoughtful. Does he care I'd never witness another dawn, hear the birds greeting the new day, or is he wondering who is this crazy woman? More wine. If he was expecting a frightened virgin, weeping and pleading for her life, he'll be proven wrong. Tonight, I will recite poetry, tell stories, sing, and dance, if needed! Just as I think more wine might help, the dark thoughts came back: Imagine your wedding night being your final night in this world! I shed a tear thinking I'll have no honeymoon, not get a chance to show off my humongous wedding ring to my girlfriends, and definitely no fancy breakfast in bed! In twenty-four hours, I'll be deflowered and beheaded. I start to lose hope, thinking maybe I should excuse myself, run to the royal bathroom, and lock myself up and make a scene, when a voice inside my head tells me, with confidence, to get my act together. "Snap out of it! Stop feeling sorry for yourself." I look around. It is my mother's voice, or, my aunts, or, the voices of the young brides murdered before me. "Come up with a plan, you miserable young thing! You come from a generation of strong women. Tell a joke, a story, offer to dance for him, or pretend to feed him but find a way to slit his throat." The voice continues, unabated, "sit up straight or you'll be a hunchback before you find a nice man! And stop drinking more wine!" I almost yell, "Mother!" before I realize I am in the presence of the powerful king. (*A pause. She appears thoughtful.*) I begin to think of all the women who have been forced into loveless marriages, kicked around, abandoned, and made to suffer. In particular, I imagine the suffering of my sisters in Iran, known to you in the West as Persia, who have been kidnapped, raped, had acid thrown on their faces, dishonored by men with swords and guns, taken as hostages by the invading Romans, the Greeks, the Mughals, the Arabs, the Turks, the Afghans, and all other foreign armies, including the British and the Russians who conquered and occupied Iran early in the twentieth century. Recalling their memories gives me courage. Look at them! *(She turns around and faces the back of stage as it gets brighter. Now the audience can see a row of women of all ages standing on a platform, behind a white lace curtain that dances with the breeze. The women smile back. One or two wipe their tears with the back of their hands. She turns around and once again addresses the audience.)* These are the ghosts of women from my land. I share their sorrow. So, I look the king in the eyes, a sin in itself, for in my culture, a king is said to be God's own shadow on earth, and ask for his permission to tell a story. The king looks surprised. He wonders whether to blame my boldness on the fine Shiraz wine, to send for the court's executioner to behead me right there and then, or, curse me when I flash my spectacular smile and flutter my long eyelashes at him. Now he is confused. He'd expected me to cry for mercy and beg for my life to be spared but not start flirting with him! You know, men are strange creatures. Then he nods, gets comfortable and with a wave of his bejeweled hand, dismisses the musicians and asks me to start.

I say a quick prayer in my head, clear my throat and, choosing my words carefully, begin to tell a story. I know many good stories by heart. I choose a long one, knowing that it'd be daylight before we get to the ending. In no time, I have him mesmerized. He watches my lips, made red with the juice from the ripe pomegranate seeds, as I tell of flying jinn, the supernatural creatures made of smokeless fire, who would turn into beautiful women ready to seduce an innocent prince and lock him up for eternity; demons who rule over lands with high mountains that serve as bedding for their tired, humongous bodies, and vast kingdoms lost over love and revenge.

Skillfully, I delay the ending to the extent that the night passes quickly. As another day is about to be born, I stop. The silence in the wedding chamber is broken by the sound of birds singing, greeting the sun. A slight breeze moves the curtains, bringing in with it the aroma of native roses. I hold my breath and, and bow in humility. I ask if his Excellency would mind postponing the ending to a later time, as sleep, like love, is one of life's necessities. The king yawns but invites me to join him in his royal bed, a bed so large, it is the size of a house where a poor family with many children can live comfortably.

The next night, once we have dined and he has had his cups of the rare wine, and I have had my sherbet made with the ice from the mountain tops, he gives me permission to tell the rest of the story. When it ends, the king, impressed with my talent, agrees to let me tell him another one. Once again, I choose a long story, delaying the ending till the day breaks gently outside. He asks me to join him in bed and we fall asleep soundly, without a care in the world.

You guessed it! My life was spared as this arrangement continued for one thousand and one nights with my starting a new story every night only to stop halfway. Impressed with my story-telling skills and reciting the right poetry at the right time, a skill so common in Iran and the Indian subcontinent, he postponed killing me in order to hear more stories. Needless to say, by now the poor man is in love with me. Me? I can live with it. I like him enough to sleep with him and make him think I love him. You see, women are skilled in art of faking love and telling good stories. It is in our DNA to make up good tales; how else would we keep restless children entertained while the men were working in the fields, off to wars, or, inside the caves, the ancient kind or the modern man caves, doing God knows what! You make up stories to distract hungry children by scaring them with stories of children-eating ghouls and wandering four-headed monsters. [*Pause.*] The moral of my story:

1. Most men are suckers for good stories! The wilder, the better!
2. Fiction can save lives. Forget what your creative writing teacher tells you.

3. There's magic in language. Words, when used correctly, and with right punctuation, could pacify a savage. But stay away from cliché!

So, my sisters, yak and yak and yak till you get what you want! And this is Scheherazade's advice for you. *(The light fades and with the stage going dark the woman walks off the stage.)*

Blackout

End of Act

Act III
The Monsters and the Mermaids

The woman in jeans and t-shirt stands on the stage facing the audience.

WOMAN: I am a poet, a woman poet from Iran, whose poetry is about oppression, witnessing, and resistance. I like to think my words give my sisters living in Iran, a land once ruled by powerful women, the voice and the platform to challenge Iran's male-dominated society. With my pen I shout, and demand justice. My voice, imprisoned and broken by my land's tradition, culture, religion, and politics, reduced to a whisper by the elders, becomes a roar, thanks to my poetry. It finds wings to reach the tarnished souls of my tired sisters. Most men dislike my poetry, for it is no longer about them and their desires, but articulates mine, as I refuse to be boxed in and labeled as a passive 'beloved' but fight to be known as a lover. That's me: the furious Persian poet on steroids! *(She smiles.)*

My poetry is the battle cry of millions of us, warning everyone that we're coming! Be afraid: unhappy sisters, tired of being locked away, as rare precious jewels, or, stored as abandoned goods, are marching down from the snow-capped mountains of Kurdistan, where they herd sheep, collect drinking water and gather firewood, and give birth to healthy babies in between! They are rushing out of factory gates where their hands, meant to give comfort to children, run the machines, to

17

make the owners rich. My sisters are walking away from the rice fields of the Caspian Sea, where with feet submerged in muddy water, they bend down for hours tending the fields. Watch out! They are coming out of rug workshops, their fingers bleeding from the long hours of weaving wool; from the homes of Shiraz, the brick buildings of Tabriz, huts of Arab Khuzestan, and tents of Turkmen, with hearts empty of romance.

I am born, die, am reborn and come to life every time a woman sighs. I am born as Rabia, the most honored Muslim saint of some fourteen centuries ago. I am Rabia of Balkh. I come back as Mahsati, the 12th century poet. I write of society's determination to keep women locked up inside their homes:

> *We can no longer be held back by the threat of arrow*
> *Or imprisoned in a gloomy cell*
> *One whose hair traps a lover, like a rope*
> *Can't be chained and kept captive indoors!*

I am persecuted for my poetry condemning religious dogma and fanaticism.
I am Tahereh, the Pure One. I was born in the nineteenth century Persia, with eyes so stunning, that I am known as Qorratol'Ayn, solace of the eye! I convert to a new religion and dare to invite the scholars to public debates. Once, in such a gathering of the new converts, being the only woman, I unveil by removing my headscarf. The men are horrified! I hear of one who cuts his own throat, preferring death to seeing

an uncovered woman! What a pity! In my life I am accused of immorality by the clergy and the king's court; though I speak of beauty, I am called ugly names. The state, terrified of the clergy's reaction, chooses to arrest me. I am 35 years-old and in prison when a guard, who is drunk, strangles me to death with my own silk scarf. I am silenced, only for a while, for I come back, in one form or another, in the body of one poet or another, to torment men with my words.

I come back as Taj Al-Saltana, a member of the Qajar dynasty, who writes, in secret, of oppression of women during her time. I am reincarnated in the bodies of many poets. I become Parvin E'tessami. I study at the American Girls College in Tehran. I am married to a cousin of my father but my marriage lasts less than three months. I write of my sisters' plight, publish a collection and die of natural causes when I am thirty-five years old.

I return as Mehrangiz Dawlatshahi, Iran's first female Ambassador, who starts a publication called *The New Way* in 1951, advocating for women's equality.

Then I come back as Simin Behbahani, the national poet of Iran, who is nominated for the Nobel Prize in literature. To describe the repressive conservative men in power in Iran, I compare them to *"monsters soaring the sky in trails of smoke, of plundered mermaids."*

I am Forough Farrokhzad. I am young, beautiful, rebellious, and a divorcee! In the late 60's Iran, I write of my lust for men, my desire to live free and not be kept in a cage like a rare bird. I make fun of women who seem content in loveless marriages that offer security and gifts of jewelry in return for obedience. I feel pity for them: made up and dressed up, like dolls, to be shown off as sport trophies. With my poetry, I challenge my society that seems ambiguous on the issue of rights for women, whether to offer or deny them the public space, let them speak for themselves or not? In Iran, it is said heaven is beneath the feet of mothers, and a fearless and independent woman is called, fondly, *shir-zan*, the lion-hearted woman. Yet the same public expects the ideal woman to be unseen. Funny enough, the word for "a woman" in Farsi, the language of Iranians, is the same as "a wife," perhaps implying that a woman's role in life is limited to being a wife! *(She sighs.)*

Forough, or, should I say I, spend time in a mental hospital, make films, fight state censorship, and publish poetry collections, including my final one, titled appropriately, *Rebirth*. When I am thirty seven, I die in a car accident. *(She pauses.)* Before I die, I write these lines, perhaps predicting my own death and rebirth:

I know a sad little nymph
Who lives inside the ocean
playing her heart
Ever so tenderly,

20

thru a small flute.
The sad little fairy,
Dies of a kiss every night
Comes to life by a kiss at dawn.

I come back, this time as Tahereh Saffarzadeh. I live a tough life; I am five when I lose both parents and am raised by my grandmother, a poet and an eye doctor herself. I get good education and get married and have a son. Later, I divorce my husband and move with my son to Tehran. After my son dies, I go to Iowa—yes, here in the U.S.!—to pursue an M.F.A. in writing. This is some forty years ago when few Iranians studied to become a writer. While in America, I get to publish *Red Umbrella*, my only poetry collection written in English. Next, I go back to Iran where I support and join the ranks of the Islamic Revolution of 1979. Voluntarily, to the dismay of my secular fellow artists, I wear the *hejab* and teach at universities in post-revolution Iran.

(*She pauses then begins speaking as if sharing a secret.*) Let me tell you something: my voice is not mine alone. No, it is not. It is the collective voice of generations of Iranian women. For example, when, in a poem, I talk of the shame my mother experienced when giving birth to me, the words could have been every woman's and the shame every mother who gave birth to a baby girl in my country. In one of my poems I pledge to return to my childhood home and wipe off the residue of shame from the walls of the room where I was born:

21

(She stands up with her back straight to recite; her voice loud and confident.)

> *It is still there, staining the room's walls*
> *my mother's shame*
> *Looking up at my father,*
> *and the grandfather*
> *once the muffled voice said,*
> *"It is a girl."*
> *Fearing no tips,*
> *For there would be no festivity*
> *Nor a circumcision*
> *the midwife shrunk to a corner.*
> *On a visit to where I was born*
> *The room where my heart began to beat*
> *I'll wash out the shame*
> *From the old walls.*

(She lowers her voice.) I feel a knot in my throat every time I hear these words. Just imagine. As we sit here, baby girls are being aborted in China, India, and so many other countries. *(She appears angry. She raises her voice.)* We get it. We're not wanted in this world! Perhaps we should say goodbye and take a leave of absence from getting pregnant and see how you'd manage without us! *(She shrugs her shoulders. Pause. She starts to speak in her normal voice.)*

My voice, as a poet, travels back and forth in time and place. It plays hide and seek with the authorities. Censorship is big in my part of the world. I am reborn as Marzieh Ahmadi Oskooii, a teacher, a leftist activist, whose poetry is about the poor and the disenfranchised in Iran. I am found guilty of giving a voice to the marginalized, the invisibles, the faceless masses, in a country that spends billions of dollars in military hardware but refuses to help the poor. My narrative is unacceptable to the State. I am murdered in 1974 by the agents of secret service working for the Shah of Iran's regime. When the bullet, made by the working people in the West, pierce through Marzieh's flesh, I, standing here in front of you today, feel the sharp pain in my body, too. My scream is lost in hers; I fall to the ground just as her young body did. We were all murdered: women who had come before us and the ones coming after us, women who worked in factories making guns and those who were killed by them. I still hear her words in my head:

I am a woman
A woman, whose significance
Is beyond your cheap vocabulary
That approves a woman
Whose manicured hands are snow white
Who has a slender figure
With soft skin,
And scented hair.
I am a woman,
Whose hands are scarred
By the sharp blades of sorrow.
One whose skin
Mirrors the desert's burning sun
And her hair
Smells of factory smoke.
I am a woman
Your storyline
has no room for me

Whose appreciation
Is missing
One in whose heart
There's rage

They murdered her along with her dreams. I look back and think, if only... *(She pauses, as if struggling to get the words out.)* If only Marzieh could have asked the king of Iran for a chance to tell him a story, just as Scheherazade did? If only she could have postponed her death, for one night, for one day, to hear the birds singing to greet the daybreak, one more time...If only she could have got another chance in life, if only, if only...

(Her voice becomes a whisper as the lights fade and the stage goes dark. A soft sound of sobbing by a lone woman gradually grows to a loud sound of wailing by a group of women.)

Blackout

End of Act

Act IV
The Veil Thingy

The WOMAN enters the stage, wearing modest Western clothes. On a small low table next to where she stands, sits a folded chador, *a* maghneh, *a* niqab, *and a headscarf. She addresses the audience.*

WOMAN: Once my mother, always the storyteller, told me the story of the public humiliation women in Iran experienced some seventy five years ago, when in 1936, Reza Shah, then Iran's king, in a rush to make Iran look modern in the eyes of the Westerners, made veiling and covering one's hair and body illegal. *(She smiles.)* You heard me right! He said no more veiling for women, forcing them, young and old, secular and conservatives, to go outside bare-headed and without a chador. *(She picks up a folded* chador *sitting on the table next to her, unfolds it and covers her hair and body with it, the way Iranian women do when they are out in the public. She speaks calmly.)*

My mother told me, with traces of old shame in her voice, how so many women, too embarrassed to be seen uncovered in public, refused to step out of their homes, and died of old age in seclusion. For centuries, Iranian women had been wearing the long piece of cloth… *(She points to the chador she's wearing.)* …which covers most of the body and hair, but not their faces. One day, you are wearing the chador, just as your mother, and her mother before them had done, and next comes the king's order, and the police rip the chador and the

25

headscarf off your head. To be fair, there were many women, those from big cities like Tehran, or those from the upper class, who liked the new mandate. To them, the choice was between modernity and tradition, and the chador was an outdated burden. My mother said there were many women who agreed with Hafiz, the fourteenth century Persian poet, when he wrote these words:

Joyful the moment, when I remove the veil off my face!

The *chadors* came off in 1936. *(She removes her* chador *and folds it neatly to place it on the table.)* What next? Fast forward to 1979, when the so-called Islamic Revolution brings the ayatollahs, the conservative turbaned men, to power and suddenly the Iranian women are told, once again by men in power, that they should start covering their hair and bodies, or face consequences, including public lashings, loss of work, and worse. Now, every woman has to be covered. *(She unfolds the* chador *and covers herself again. She shakes her head in disbelief.)* I ask the men in Iran this simple question: *(She raises her voice as if speaking to an unseen group of people.)* "Can you make up your mind? First, you tell women to unveil for sake of modernity, then, some sixty years later, you tell them they have to cover for sake of Islam. Really!" *(She removes her* chador *and looks frustrated.)* Would you make up your mind?

(She looks to her right and left and lowers her voice.) What if, and I risk being arrested by the moral police for saying this, what if, men in Iran were to be blindfolded when in public so that seeing my hair and body curves, would not make them lose control and make them commit the sin of desiring sex outside of marriage? Is that asking for too much? Or, I have a better idea. What if they'd turn into stone, whenever they look at women in lust? *(She smiles and looks excited.)* I've got to admit I'd rather see a city of dusty men, frozen for eternity, for having sinful thoughts, than watch a bunch of women walking around, covered in black, who look like crows. *(She laughs loudly.)* Think about it. Do the men deserve to go to paradise, if they are that weak and unwilling to control their urges?

But... *(She sighs.)* ... men are not the only ones to blame. There are women in Iran, and elsewhere, who would hate me for not wearing a headscarf. Still worse, those who would dislike me for wearing one! Listen to this! In the West, most feel sorry for me when they see me keeping *hejab. (She wears a scarf in the way Muslim women do in the West.)* You all judge me, sometimes behind my back, some with your hostile looks, thinking of me as an oppressed woman, as a submissive Muslim female, all because I am covering my head with a piece of cloth. Here in the university where I study, every now and then, a female professor takes me inside her office and tells me, with confidence, that I do not have to wear the *hejab,* that here in the West, I am free to decide for myself, that I could remove my veil, if I choose to do so. I stand there listening and not saying a word. How am I to tell this kind-hearted, but misguided woman, a person of my gender, who should know better than to make assumptions and judge others before asking a few questions, that I wear my *hejab* with pride, that I do so out of my love for my faith, that I might be doing so to tell the world I am a Muslim woman and proud of being one? I stand there saying nothing. How am I to challenge her way of thinking, that says young women should not be religious, that because of her personal experience, she believes that faith traditions, be they Judaism, Islam, Hinduism, Sikhism, and so on, have no room for women? I am damned for not wearing *hejab*, cursed and threatened by religious conservatives, and damned for wearing it, judged harshly by the secular Muslims and secular Westerners.

Look at me. *(Elaborately, she removes the headscarf, replacing it with a* neqab.*)* I'm still the same person. I'm the same person with or without the veil! Look me in the eyes, and try to see a human being behind this mask. Judge me for who I am and not what I choose to wear, or, have been asked to wear. Stop, please stop, staring at me when you see me at the park, in the mall, or at the university cafeteria. Stop feeling sorry for me, thinking my father or my husband has forced me to wear this scarf. That can be the case with many, many Muslim women, young and old, but there are some of us, who want to cover ourselves. We cannot all be the victims you make us to be. I am not, I assure you, oppressed because I wear a scarf.

(She walks forward toward the audience, removes the niqab and raises her voice.) Millions of my sisters are forced to stay at home, stop their education, silenced and pushed to the society's edge for being a woman. Many men in power—the Taliban, the ayatollahs, the emirs, some sheikhs—claim to speak for God when it comes to women's rights when, in truth, they are speaking for their own bias. They fear education so they blow up girls schools; they fear change, so they make women stop working outside of their home. They mistake cultural, tribal, political, and traditional forces for religious teaching and call it Islam. But God in Islam is gender-neutral. As a woman, I do not believe my gender has anything to do with my piety. But Muslim men run the show. They act as telephone operators for God, free to interpret as they wish and pass along only the information that suits them. Some would say women have no place in Islam, ignoring the historical facts and that Islam offers women the right to marry, divorce, inherit and own property. The Qur'an says it clearly: "We created you from a single soul, and a blood clot!" It says nothing of men being superior to women. But in the West, some would believe the false story, the story that the sexist telephone operators have offered. Then, you'd talk of rescuing the helpless Muslim women and you might send your army and marines to Muslim lands to save women from the bad Muslim wolf. How about supporting us in finding our voices? Not all Muslim women are sitting and waiting to be saved. Here's an idea: Have your government build schools and health clinics in Muslim lands, train our young women to

become social workers, nurses, teachers and doctors. Send us your teachers and doctors instead of tanks and drones. We have stories to tell each other. We share our collective sorrow in seeing our men, and women, killing each other in the name of fighting the War on Terror.

(She sighs.) Now I am exhausted! *(She smiles and lowers her voice.)* Let me tell you something: as a woman, I am tired of being judged for covering my hair, asked to uncover, straighten my hair, wear scanty clothes, bare my body to sell alcohol, be enticed to get a boob job, shrink my nose, fatten my lips, get rid of my wrinkles, shave my armpits, lose weight, look hot, act sexy, and wear high heels and makeup, all to meet the society's expectations. Perhaps you can relate? This is unattainable.

(She pauses, looks thoughtful as if searching for a thought. She wears the headscarf again.) Here is the deal: I cover my hair, you wear a short skirt or a long one, or, a pair of pants, if you like; bare your arms, shave or don't shave your legs, and we call it even. Deal? Let me be who I am, and I won't judge you for your unconscious efforts to fill up the businessmen's pockets by buying their beauty products, their Victoria's not so-secret tiny garments, and helping them set the beauty standards for you and your daughters, and me and my daughters, making women everywhere feel inadequate for failing to look like teen models! We all have work to do. Our humanity is what connects us. As sisters, we have battles to

win and hearts and minds to change. We could look at each other as Muslims, seculars, atheists, Christians, Westerners, Jews, illegal immigrants, gays, Republicans, blacks, and treat one another as the Other, through the barrels of guns. Or, we could come together as sisters, mothers, daughters, and women of the world. Don't judge me, and I won't judge you. Love me, and I'll love you back. Wipe my tears, and I'll do the same for you. We have so much work to do together... *(The stage goes dark as she leaves.)*

Blackout

End of Act

Act V
The Assassin and the Daughter of Revolution

The young woman enters the stage. She is wearing jeans and t-shirt. She drops her backpack on the floor, takes a deep breath and begins to speak.

YOUNG WOMAN: Hi there! Halloween or not, I am a ghost! Here I am: a ghost with stories to tell. Whose ghost? A fair question: I'm the ghost of Neda, the young Iranian woman who was murdered during the 2009 street demonstrations protesting the presidential election results in Iran. Don't worry if you did not hear of my fate. I am here to tell you the whole story: I was born during the 1979 Islamic Revolution of Iran. That would make me as old as the revolution itself. My life began amidst the familiar noises of the revolution: the chaotic sounds of machine-gun fire, the earth-shaking bomb blasts, and the shouting of slogans by the demonstrators, the nation's collective sense of fear and uncertainty. My mother and my country went through the discomfort and pain of pregnancy together; one giving birth to me and the other to the revolution. I am a child of the uprising of 1979 that brought to power the bearded ayatollahs—the men who claim to speak for God.

As the anti-western revolution matured, I was taught to hate America, Israel, Saddam Hussein's Iraq, England, Russia, England, and others. While a student, we started each school day with shouting "Death to America!" I had no idea why we had to hate Americans, but we were told the Satanic America was responsible for Saddam's invasion of Iran in 1980 and the resulting miseries including the shortages in food and fuel. As children we learned to practice ducking under our desks, should bombs made by Americans and dropped by Iraqis hit the school building.

Most days, our backpacks… *(She points to hers sitting on the floor next to her.)* were searched by our teachers. They looked for cassette tapes of Michael Jackson's music, copies of banned poetry books, and bottles of nail polish, all considered contraband and tools of the Western Imperialism. *(She smiles and lowers her voice.)* Once I hid Forough Farrokhzad's collection of poetry wrapped in the covers of my Algebra textbook and got away with reading it at school! How can you imprison poetry?

Out in the streets and neighborhoods, "Brothers," as we now called the bearded men carrying guns and acting as government vigilante, went around harassing men and women who did not look "Islamic" enough. They arrested women for failing to cover their bodies and hair in accordance with the state's strict dress code. Once I was slapped across my face, by a woman vigilante, for wearing colorful socks and western-looking sneakers.

Life was tough. We watched mourners wailing at the loss of their sons, and daughters, to the monstrous Iran-Iraq War. My childhood was in black and gray. There were no colors. As a child, I imagined the birds having abandoned the skies, as I could no longer hear them sing. I am a child of a revolution that murdered imagination, hope, and beauty. As a young girl, I imagined most men to be monsters, bloodthirsty and wicked creatures, and my only chance of protection against them was to be covered in black and be void of any feminine beauty.

The same revolution that gave birth to me had me murdered by an assassin hired by the same regime. In the summer of 2009, when the youth in Iran took to the streets to challenge the conservative mullah's alleged stealing of the presidential election, I was there with them as the daughter of a revolution that had turned its back on the people. The assassin's bullet flew through the charged air of a street, named Worker Street in Tehran, to find my throat, to silence me, and my fellow protesters.

(She pauses. Long silence. Then she begins with a sad smile.) It is funny how the words "assassin" and "assassination" came to English from Farsi, the language we speak in Iran. Don't get me wrong; we gave the English language some sweet and delicious words too: candy, sugar, orange to name a few.

As a child, I heard tales from the One Thousand and One Night, told by Scheherazade, the storyteller. Most tales dealt with betrayal, tyranny, love and sorrow taking place in the ancient cities of Baghdad, Cairo, Damascus, Samarkand, Bukhara, et cetera. That's where I heard about the assassins:

men who used to climb the walls of palaces, forts, and private homes to kill the enemies of their masters. The term "assassin" comes from the Farsi word *"hashishian,"* for the killers got high on hashish, a popular narcotic, before going out to kill under the darkness of night.

But it was in bright daylight, on a street in Tehran, right in front of a crowd, that an assassin killed me. As I died, I understand, someone took a picture of me, bleeding and dying, on their smart phone and sent it to others. The world, I hear, got to see my young face, with eyes wide open, dying, saying good bye to the sun and the sky. The image stained the collective memory of Iranians, young and old, as it travelled around the world. I know it reached you, as you sat comfortably in your living room, worrying about something as mundane as who'd become the next American Idol, or, Kim Kardashian's divorce, or, if feminism as a social force had died a natural death. No hard feelings if you failed to pay attention to the unsuccessful youth-led protests in Iran. Now many believe these same protests gave birth to the Arab Spring of later years.

(She pauses, and lowers her head. Next she stares into the space, as if trying to remember something. She begins speaking in a softer voice.) Did you know after I died, a street in Italy was named after me? In Holland, oh, but first let me tell you something about that country. *(She closes her eyes and with folded hands, as if praying, she begins talking.)* How

I wished to go to Holland and visit Amsterdam at least once in my lifetime, to sit in a café by the canal, next to one of the old bridges, to sip coffee, and hold my lover's hand. You see, in today's Iran, the young members of the opposite sex, unless married or related to each other, cannot be seen together in public. How I wanted to hold my lover's hand and walk around, feeling free and without a shame! But as I was saying, in Holland, a postal stamp showing my face, smiling innocently, was issued by their government. What a nice thing to do!

But, I wonder how much the world knew and cared about the young men and women who died during the anti-government demonstration in 2009, or, the hundreds who still sit in prison cells in Iran? There were millions of us who came out to the streets to protest the stealing of our votes by the mullahs. We were unarmed. We walked in silence, refusing to call for violence against the mullahs, or, be provoked to do so. We simply wanted our votes, our hopes, and futures back. Was that asking for too much?

I was there as a university student, a divorcee, a child of the same revolution that jailed and killed its opponents. What the Islamic revolution accomplished in 1979 Revolution was this: one form of tyranny replacing another, the turban replacing the crown. The assassin's bullet found me. Fearful of my voice, my clenched fist, they murdered me, for despite all their guns, their dark dungeons, and torture chambers, they are frightened by the youth, and our desire for freedom.

My name is Neda, or it can be Iran-dokht, or, Shaherzad, or, Tahereh, or, Forough.

(Here characters from the previous scenes can join the woman on stage, taking turns walking to the center of the stage to say their names.)

FIRST ACTOR: Indeed, I am Eve. I am related to all the saints, and yet, many say I caused the fall of Adam. Christianity blames me for causing all sins. Because of one single apple, I am cursed for eternity. Because of my gender, all women are cursed for eternity. The Muslim fundamentalists punish my female off-springs by forcing them to cover their bodies, their hair, and skin. To them, modern women might cause the fall of men by showing their hair and baring their skin. In their eyes, my hair represents the apple and my curvy body resembles the snake. Never mind that Islam disagrees with the Christian notion of Eve's guilt. In Islam, the blame for the fall of man is shared equally between Eve and Adam. But few Muslims are that knowledgeable about their own faith!

SECOND ACTOR: My name is Eve, or, I might be a descendent of the Prophet's own wife, who was the first person to accept Islam, when the latest Abrahamic faith was born fourteen hundred years ago. I could be related to the Prophet's daughter, who accompanied her father in battles to defend Islam against its early enemies. But the assassin is deaf and blind. He bears no witness to history, reads no poetry, and sees no traces of Eve, Rabia, other women saints, the Prophet's wife or his daughter in me. The assassin is blind and indifferent to my beauty. He curses women bitterly because he has forgotten the sweet whispers of love lullabies mouthed by his own mother. He is deaf and hears no holy verses commanding him to respect me, as a woman. He says to me, speaking the language of violence, through his bullet, which is aimed at my throat, where the shouts of one thousand and one other women have been trapped, "I'll silence you, you infidel whore!" I smile back and whisper, as I die, with the world watching my dying, "My ghost will haunt your memory, and that of your masters, who arm you and send you out to beat, maim and kill women and men activists."

THIRD ACTOR: My name is Neda. I am of the flesh and blood of all women martyrs. Although dead, I live inside the hearts of young girls, who dream of a world where sexual violence against women, honor killing and bride burning are meaningless terms, retired to the dictionary, where tyrants exist just in stories read at bedtime. I give courage to a girl to leave her home to walk to a school that is targeted by criminals, who believe in depriving half of their society of the gift of education. I bring the love of learning and story-telling to the hearts of young girls in Kurdistan, Azerbaijan,

Baluchistan, and every part of Iran. Where do I live? I occupy the heads of male assassins and their masters, just to torment them.

FOURTH ACTOR: I have other stories to tell you: tales of loss, unfulfilled love and shattered dreams. I am a woman who dances softly to the music of the gentle rain falling on the Caspian Sea. I sleep in the stillness of Kurdistan's snow-covered valleys, and wake up to the desert winds of Kerman, in south of Iran. [*Pause. She yawns.*] But I see the daylight breaking outside. A new day is coming. Darkness gives in to light. I have to stop here and leave the ending, happy or not, for a later time. I'll be back with more stories, I promise. I have seen and heard a great deal in this lifetime of mine. I have much to say.

ALL: *(Speaking in unison.)* So, I ask you to wait for me, to make room in your dream for me. Do not forget my name, for I'll be back, I promise. Wait for me…I have so much more to say. *(The light fades. The ACTORS continue to whisper words which can no longer be heard. The soft Iranian music can be heard as the stage goes dark.)*

Blackout

End of Play

APPENDIX

Timeline

1870's	Iranian Muslim girls are admitted to the school established by American missionaries in Tehran.
1906-1911	Constitutional Revolution (a national movement to curb the king's power).
1907	The first women associations are established, in Tehran. They include Women's Association for Freedom and Women's Secret Union.
1910	Publication of *Danesh* (Knowledge), Iran's first women's journal.
1911	Establishment of girls' schools.
1918	First Teacher Education College for girls is opened.
1921	Reza Khan, a military commander, seizes power.
1922	Mohtaram Eskandari, an activist, helps to found the Patriotic Women League. She is condemned by some religious elders and is arrested.
1924	First public performance by Qamar ol-Moluk Vaziri. She sings at Tehran's Grand Hotel.
1925	The last Qajar dynasty monarch is deposed. Reza Khan is named the new Shah.

1926	After her return from the International Women's Conference in Paris, France, Sedigheh Dowlatabadi appears unveiled in public.
1928	Women can get financial assistance to study abroad.
1933	First Iranian-made film to feature a female actor is shown in cinemas.
1935	Women are admitted to university.
1935	Reza Shah changes the country's name from Persia to Iran.
1936	The new law requires women to appear in public unveiled.
1941	Reza Shah is forced by the Allied Powers to abdicate in favor of his son, Mohammed Reza Pahlavi (Shah of Iran).
1942	Dr Fatemeh Sayyah becomes Iran's first woman professor.
1947	Mehrangiz Manuchehrian becomes Iran's first female lawyer.
1950	Dr. Mohammed Mosaddegh, a popular nationalist, becomes prime minister.
1951	Mehrangiz Dawlatshahi starts publishing *The New Way,* to advocate for women's equality.

1951	Nationalization of the oil industry by Mosaddegh's government.
1953	Shah flees, leaving Iran for exile.
1953	In August, Mosaddegh's government is toppled by a military coup, staged by the British and American governments. Shah returns to his throne.
1958	Sattareh Farman-Farmaian establishes Iran's first School of Social Work.
1963	As part of the White Revolution, initiated by the Shah on advice from the U.S. government, Iranian women are given the right to vote.
1963	For the first time, six women are elected to the *Majles.*
1967	The Family Protection Act is passed.
1968	Farookhro Parsa becomes Iran's first woman to act as the minister of education (She is executed in the post-Islamic Revolution Iran).
1971	Mehrnoush Ebrahimi, a leftist activist, becomes the first Iranian woman to be killed by the SAVAK, the Shah's security police.
1975	Mahnaz Afkhami becomes the minister for the newly-established ministry of women's affairs.
1976	Iran sends a female ambassador to Denmark.

1977   Abortion is made legal for unmarried women. Married women would require their husbands' consent for an abortion.

1978   Strikes, riots and massive anti-Shah demonstrations take place across Iran. Protesters are killed by the army. Martial law is imposed.

1979   The Shah and his family leave. Ayatollah Khamenei returns to Iran, after nearly fifteen years in exile. The military announces its neutrality, causing the collapse of Shah's regime, and monarchy in Iran. On April 1, following a national referendum, the Islamic Republic of Iran replaces the old regime. The emergence of the National Union of Women.

1979   The Constitution of the Islamic Republic of Iran is drafted. Article 3 of the Constitution gives Iranian women the right to free education, employment, and equality before the law. However, these rights are subject to "conformity with Islamic law."

1980   Four women are elected to the first post-revolution *Majlis,* Parliament.

1980   Iraqi forces invade Iran, resulting in the start of Iran-Iraq War. The post-revolution regime becomes repressive. Arrests, imprisonments, and executions of regime's opponents, members of religious and ethnic minorities begin. Women's rights are diminished; right to divorce and child custody are reduced, women cannot serve as judges.

1982   All educational institutions, with the exception of universities, become gender segregated.

1983   Veiling becomes mandatory. Iranian women, young and old, can no longer appear unveiled, in public. The *Qesas,* the Bill of Retributions, becomes law. It provides, among others, for punishing of women by public lashing for failure to observe veiling, lowering the legal status of a woman to half of a man, and stoning women for adultery.

1983-84   Due to high inflation and shortages, caused by the war with Iraq, and the loss of male soldiers during the conflict, women have to join the labor force in large numbers.

1985   The first women religious studies center is established in the holy city of Qom.

1988   Iran-Iraq War ends. The state changes some of its policies in regard to women by removing some of the restrictions. State-funded family planning programs are introduced.

1992   Women are appointed as advisory judges. An influential women's magazine, *Zanan* (Women) is managed and published by the well-known activist, Shahla Sherkat. The journal advocates a brand of feminism that is inspired, and takes its legitimacy, from Islam.

1996   Fourteen women are elected to the *Majlis.*

1996   For the first time since the Islamic Revolution, women athletes compete publicly.

1997   The reformist Mohammad Khatami wins the presidential election, in part, with support from women.

1997   Simin Behbahani, Iran's most popular poet is nominated for the Nobel Prize in Literature.

1997   Masoumeh Ebtekar, Ph.D. becomes Iran's first female vice-president during the President Khatami's administration.

1998   Eighteen-year-old Samira Makhmalbaf becomes world's youngest director to participate in the Cannes Film Festival.

Two years later, she wins the Jury Prize for her second feature film, *The Blackboard*.

2000   For the first time since the revolution, activists gather in Tehran to celebrate the International Women's Day.

2000   Out of 5,723 candidates during the elections to the *Majlis*, 417 are women.

2001   Khatami is re-elected to a second term.

2002   According to the official data, 60 percent of university students are women.

2003   Human rights activist and lawyer, Shirin Ebadi becomes the first Iranian to win the Nobel Peace Prize.

2005	Mahmoud Ahmadinejad, an ultra-conservative, wins the presidential election.
2006	A coalition of secular and Muslim feminists launch the Campaign for One Million Signatures.
2006	Anousheh Ansari, an American-Iranian investor, becomes the first Iranian, and a Muslim, woman to travel to the International Space Station.
2009	Iranian citizens protest the disputed presidential election results, which give the presidency to Ahmadinejad. They accuse the hardliners of election fraud. Street demonstrations rock Iran's major cities, including Tehran. Thousands of protesters are arrested and dozens are killed, including Neda Agha Soltan, a 26-year-old student. Her death became an international symbol for the popular anti-regime undertaking, the Green Movement.
2010	An Iranian woman is stoned to death, causing international condemnation.
2013	Reformist-backed Hassan Rouhani wins presidential election.
2013	Well-known human rights activist, Nasrin Sotoudeh, is released from prison. Her Unjust imprisonment had caused international outcry.

The Poets

Rabia of Balkh of the 10th century medieval Persia was born in a royal family. She is believed to be the first woman poet to write love poetry in modern Persian language. Rabia is known for her tragic love affair with a Turkish servant. Once her brother, who ruled the land, heard of their secret, he condemned her to death. To this day, young couples gather at her tomb to pray and pay homage to love.

Mahsati (1089-1159) is known for writing quatrains, or, *rubaiyat*, and having been a companion of Omar Khayyam. Her alleged love affairs, controversial poetry praising the richness of love, and condemning religious fanaticism, made her a target of persecution during her lifetime.

Tahereh (1814–1852), also known as "Qurrat al-'Ayn" (Solace of the Eyes), is revered as a saint in the Bábí and Bahá'í faiths and recognized for articulating the women emancipation movement in ancient Persia. She was born into a religious family and was educated by her father in theology, literature, and philosophy. In 1852, she was sentenced to death, as a heretic.

Taj Al-Saltana (1884-1936) was the daughter of Naser al-Din Shah, a Qajar king. She received partial education within the harem walls of the royal palace and was married when thirteen years-old. In her 1914 memoir, *Crowning Anguish,* she is critical of the exploitation of women and the socioeconomic problems that existed in her country. Additionally, her recollections describe a woman's sexual and political awakening in the early-twentieth century Iran.

Parvin E'tessami (1907–1941) composed her first poem in classical style and contributed regularly to her father's magazine, *Bahār.* She studied at the American Girls College in Tehran. Her marriage ended in divorce. Her first collection of poems was published in 1935. She was only thirty-five when she died of Typhoid fever.

Simin Behbahani (1927-2014) is the most prominent Iranian poet. Known as Iran's national poet, she was nominated twice for the Nobel Prize in literature. Her poetry collections include *The Broken Lute, Footprint, Candelabrum, Marble, Resurrection, A Line of Speed and Fire, Arzhan Plain, Paper Dress,* and *A small Window of freedom.*

Forough Farrokhzad (1935-1967) was an Iranian poet, a feminist, and a film director. She is one of Iran's most influential female poets of the twentieth century. Forough married her cousin at age sixteen and was divorced after three years, resulting in loss of the custody of her only child. Her collections include *The Captive, The Wall, Rebellion,* and *Rebirth.* A few years after her death in a car accident in 1967, *Let Us Believe in the Beginning of the Cold Season* was published.

Tahereh Saffarzadeh (1936-2008) was a poet, translator, Muslim feminist, and a university professor. She received her M.F.A. from the University of Iowa. In 1969, while still in the U.S., she published *Red Umbrella*, her only collection of poetry written in English. She has published fourteen volumes of poems, in addition, to a few translations of the Qur'an.

Marzieh Ahmadi Oskooii (1945-1974) was a graduate of Teachers' College in Iran. She was a member of the People's Democratic Front, a Leftist group opposing the Shah's regime. She was killed in an armed confrontation with the agents of the Iranian secret police, SAVAK.